Copyright © 2002 by Michael Neugebauer Verlag,
an imprint of Nord-Süd Verlag AG, Gossau Zürich, Switzerland
First published in Switzerland under the title Der Schneerabe
English translation copyright © 2002 by North-South Books Inc., New York

First published in the United States, Great Britain, Canada,
Australia, and New Zealand in 2002 by North-South Books,
an imprint of Nord-Süd Verlag AG, Gossau Zürich, Switzerland.

Distributed in the United States by North-South Books Inc., New York.

Library of Congress Cataloging-in-Publication Data is available.
A CIP catalogue record for this book is available from The British Library.
ISBN 0-7358-1689-1 (trade edition) 10 9 8 7 6 5 4 3 2 1
ISBN 0-7358-1690-5 (library edition) 10 9 8 7 6 5 4 3 2 1
Printed in Italy

For more information about our books, and the authors and artists who
create them, visit our web site: www.northsouth.com

SNOW
RAVENS

Illustrated by Birte Müller

By Bruno Hächler

Translated by Marianne Martens

A Michael Neugebauer Book
NORTH-SOUTH BOOKS
New York / London

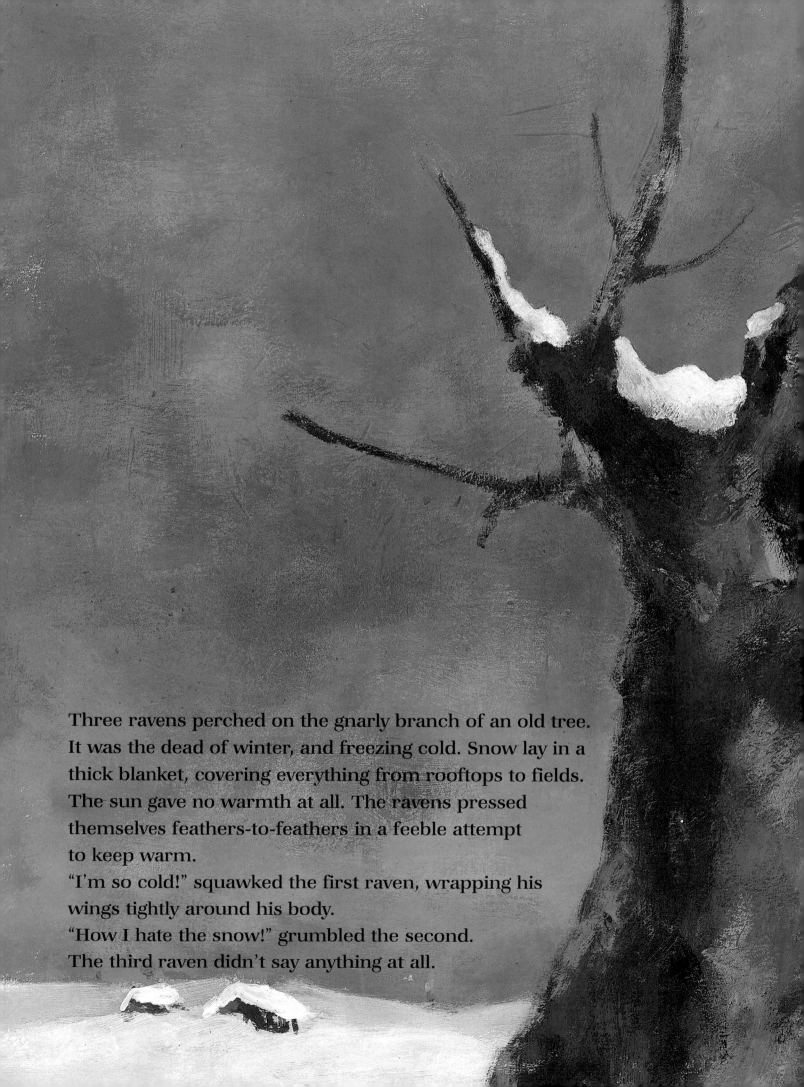

Three ravens perched on the gnarly branch of an old tree.
It was the dead of winter, and freezing cold. Snow lay in a
thick blanket, covering everything from rooftops to fields.
The sun gave no warmth at all. The ravens pressed
themselves feathers-to-feathers in a feeble attempt
to keep warm.

"I'm so cold!" squawked the first raven, wrapping his
wings tightly around his body.

"How I hate the snow!" grumbled the second.

The third raven didn't say anything at all.

"White, white, nothing but white everywhere,"
croaked the first raven, dreaming of golden cornfields
dotted with red poppies.
"How depressing," agreed the second, thinking of the sweet cherries
he liked to eat in the summertime.
The third raven didn't say anything at all.
Shyly, he peeked at the children and heard their giggles as they stomped
around in the field. He thought it might be fun to play with them.
"Brrrrrrr," whimpered the first raven.
"Oh, woe," whined the second one.
The third raven didn't say anything at all.

So there they sat. One hour passed. Then two
hours. Then the whole afternoon drifted by.
At one point, a pile of snow plopped down
on their heads from the branch above.
The first two ravens complained loudly.
The third raven just chuckled, imagining
that the snow on his head was a crown.

Suddenly, the ravens heard shouting and cheering.
"How can those children be so loud!" said the first raven.
"So unbelievably loud," agreed the second.
The third raven peeked curiously down
to see what the children were doing.

How strange. The children were lying on their backs
in the snow, waving their arms and legs as if they were
wings. "Look at my snow angel!" they shouted, standing
up to admire the figures they had made in the snow.
I would love to try that, thought the third raven.

The sun was setting by the time the children headed for home. The raven stretched his damp limbs and flew off. Gently, he landed on the field.

He tried all sorts of things. He pressed his feathery belly into the snow, spread his wings, wiggled his tail. He jumped up and down and spun in a circle. Impossible. His snow prints looked more like moles or elephants or kangaroos—anything but angels.

But the raven didn't give up. He flapped his wings even harder, jumped higher in the air, spun in a circle, and each time he landed, he made even crazier shapes in the snow. At last he landed flat on his back with his wings spread far out to the sides. He couldn't get back up.

From the tree above him, he heard snickering. "Look down there," said the first raven.

"Looks like a bird swimming on his back," said the second raven. They laughed for a long time.

The third raven felt a little bit embarrassed. Quietly, he lay there in the snow.

Finally the other two ravens flew down and helped him up.

The next morning the third raven sat by himself on the tree branch. Before long some children appeared. Happily they stomped around the field and began to play. Suddenly they noticed the brand-new teeny-tiny print in the snow. It was such a sweet little image—so delicate. There could be no doubt—

"It must have been made by a real angel!" the children declared.

The raven felt very proud—so proud that he didn't even notice that it had begun to snow.

White flakes landed on his black feathers, and soon he was completely white.

Just then, one of the children saw the raven sitting in the tree. "Look!" he cried. "It's the tiny angel!"

Eyes shining, the children stared in wonder.

Above them, the raven took a deep breath,
threw back his head, and let out a loud long
caw that echoed joyfully in the cold winter air.